Susanne Wolf

Adventurous Abby

A Daring Young Dog

Illustrated by Theresa Werner

Printing and Production: BoD - Books on Demand, Norderstedt

ISBN 978-3-7526-6943-5

Translated from German into English by: Twigg's Translations
www.twigg.de

For my Abby

The little husky girl Abby lives together with her whole family on top of a mountain surrounded by meadows and forests. Her family is made up of her husky parents, her sister and three brothers, an aunt, an uncle and, of course, the humans they live with. The humans are a family – mum Susan, dad James and the two children Sophie and Nick. Everyone loves Abby because she's always happy and friendly. What's more, she's the cutest pup you could ever imagine. She can be a little clumsy and mischievous too, but you still can't help but adore her. Abby's owners love her to bits; Sophie and her mum, in particular, are simply crazy about her.
Abby and her family really enjoy living on the mountain. They have lots of space for running and romping around. Their owners take them for long walks and, in the winter, they love to pull James on his sledge through the snow-covered landscape – like all real sledge dogs.
The rest of the day is spent playing or just being lazy.

This is what it looks like when Abby and the other huskies are pulling James' sledge.

Abby loves lying on top of her kennel in the garden and gazing down into the valley. Sometimes she imagines what it would be like to explore the forest all by herself, without her owners.

What adventures she would have!

Today, like most other days, Abby is dozing on top of her kennel, when suddenly she hears the faintest of sounds, barely audible even for a dog's amazing sense of hearing. Sleepily, she opens her eyes. 
A little fox is trying to get into the garden through a hole in the fence that is hidden by shrubs.
Abby takes a quick look around to check that none of the other dogs is nearby. Satisfied that she's alone, she slowly and cautiously approaches the little fox who's still trying to squeeze his way through. Seeing his frightened face, Abby says in a soft voice, "Hello little fox. You needn't be scared of me, but what are doing here? I have three brothers, you know. Although they're actually really nice, two of them are pretty wild ruffians and you wouldn't want to get caught by them in our garden."

The little fox worms his way out of the hole, back to the other side of the fence. Still looking terrified, he whispers to Abby in the tiniest of voices, "I had no idea this was your property. But you see, just a short while ago I saw a wolf down in the valley and I really didn't want to come face to face with him."
The little fox looks anxiously all around, but there is no wolf to be seen. Laughing, Abby replies, "I'm sure it was just a dog you saw. Most people say my Uncle Max looks like a wolf. But there haven't been any wolves in this area for over a hundred years."
"You can believe what you want," answers the fox, "but I'm certain it was a wolf. Besides, there are more hunters and other people than usual roaming around in our forest. I should hurry back home to my family. My name is Tim, by the way. You seem very nice. Maybe we'll see each other again sometime."

Tim runs off as fast as his paws can carry him.

Abby shakes her head in wonder. What a crazy little fox Tim is, she thinks to herself as she lies back down on top of her kennel and continues her nap.

Suddenly, however, a thought springs to her mind. What if she uses this newfound hole in the fence to go out into the forest? The hole will be my secret, she thinks.

None of the other dogs, and not even the humans, know about the hole. James would have repaired it long ago had he known about it. Abby thinks long and hard.

Her owners mustn't notice that she's gone, otherwise they would worry themselves to bits and Abby certainly doesn't want that to happen.

But soon she can't contain her excitement any longer. Adventure awaits!

Abby chooses the perfect moment. The other dogs have just eaten and now they're all napping.
She creeps stealthily over to the fence, squeezes through the small hole and before she knows it she's on the other side. She quickly runs away from the garden, following a path she already knows. Her heart is pounding. She's never been off on her own before.

First, Abby follows the route she's
walked many times with Sophie or
Susan.
But this time she's not on a lead.
She can leave the path and sniff to her
heart's content wherever she chooses.

She loves this new feeling of freedom.

Abby knows the vast area around her home well and is not worried about getting lost.
First, she decides, she'd like to go for a swim in the nearby lake.
When she has almost reached the lake, she hears voices. She creeps forward quietly and sees a family with two children swimming in the water. At the edge of the lake she spots a large basket packed with tasty things to eat. These people must be planning to have a picnic, she thinks.

Not wanting to be discovered, Abby decides to postpone her swim and, instead, to run all the way through the forest to a little cave. She and Sophie often hide there when they're out on a walk with the family. Then James and Susan have to find them.
But when she's out with Sophie, they always follow proper paths. And now Abby realises that cutting straight through the forest is much harder.

Tired, she finally makes it to the cave. Filled with glee, she runs towards it but stops at the last moment outside the entrance and peers cautiously inside. Staring out at her from the darkness are two bright eyes.

Now Abby starts to feel a little scared. Never before has she seen such a piercing gaze. In a trembling voice she whispers, "Hello, my name is Abby. Who are you?"

"My name is Tala," whispers a friendly yet anxious voice back. "I'm hiding here from the humans. You see, I got separated from my pack. I so want to return to the others."
Abby summons up all her courage and steps into the dark cave. Once her eyes have become accustomed to the darkness, she sees that Tala is indeed a wolf. Fear washes over Abby. She has heard so many horror stories about wolves. Tala notices the look of fright on Abby's face and says softly, "Little husky Abby, don't be scared of me. I won't hurt you. I know some people tell terrible stories about us wolves, but humans really don't know us. They're frightened of us because they don't understand how we live. To them, we are wild, dangerous, mysterious creatures. But we too live together as a family; we take care of one another. Can you help me find my way back?"
Abby is still a little frightened – the wolf is, after all, much bigger than she is. But her gentle words reassure Abby. Tala seems very nice, and maybe Abby really can help her.
"OK," says Abby softly. "I'll help you if I can. But where are you from? Where is your pack?"

Tala explains that she and her brother wandered far too far away from the rest of their pack because they wanted to explore the great, wide world. They walked for a very long time until they came to a wide river. While they were looking for something to eat, Tala fell off a rocky ledge into the water and hit her head on a rock. She became unconscious and was washed downstream. A short time later, she woke up on the other side of the river. Some humans spotted her, and now they were trying to hunt her down. Luckily, she found this hiding place in the cave, but now she has to return to the river.

Abby remembers Tim, the little fox. He was telling the truth all along. He really did see a wolf. Now Abby starts to wonder if this was a good idea after all, to leave her safe home and wander through the forest. Hopefully I won't end up in a situation like Tala, she thinks to herself. Abby wishes she were back home. But right now Tala needs help and Abby wants to do all she can. "Tala," she says, "I may not be a wolf like you, but I know my way around here very well. I know how to get to the river, and I even know a spot where you can cross it safely. But we have to set off straight away. I want to return home as quickly as possible too. We'll have to be very careful since it seems that several humans are on the look-out for you. I don't think they would shoot you, but they will surely try to catch you. Then they would put you in a wildlife park."

"That would be the worst possible thing that could happen," gasps Tala. "I could never live in captivity. I so want to return to my pack. I'm very relieved to have met you and that you're helping me. But I'm also incredibly hungry. I haven't eaten anything in days."

"Good, then let's set off," says Abby quietly. "It's not very far, but we have to be on our guard. And, Tala, we're going to make a little detour on the way to the river."

Running as fast as she can, Abby leads Tala along hidden trails to the little lake. She has a plan for getting her wolf friend something to eat. When they reach the lake, Tala hides a short distance away in some bushes, while Abby creeps stealthily up to the lake. The whole family is in the water giving Abby the perfect opportunity to sneak up to the picnic basket on the shore. She peeks in. Just as she thought – tasty chicken wings and schnitzels. Abby takes as much as she can carry in her mouth and slips away unnoticed by the family. Once they are a safe distance away, Tala eats until she is full. Abby, who normally can't resist such delicious treats, eats only a tiny amount. Her new friend needs it more than she does.

But now it's time for them to embark on the dangerous walk to the river. Abby leads Tala through the forest. There are no hunters or other humans to be seen or heard anywhere. They make good progress. They're not far from the river now. Suddenly a raven flies over their heads. "You two are a funny pair," he caws. "I've heard about you, the husky helping the wolf. But humans are out looking for you, wolf. Some of them are near the river. Be as quiet as you can and take the short-cut through the long cave. There's a passageway through the cave with a small exit at the end. It'll take you almost all the way to the river."
"Thank you, dear raven," replies Abby. "But I'm not sure where the entrance to the cave is. Can you lead us there?"

The raven says he'd be delighted to help such a brave little husky and her wolf friend and tells them to follow him.

He flies ahead of them and a short while later they reach the entrance to the great, long cave. He wishes them good luck before flying away.

Abby and Tala walk into the cave and follow the long, dark passageway that should take them almost all the way to the bank of the river.
It's very dark in the cave. The two friends can't even see their own paws. They edge ahead slowly. Abby is scared in the darkness. The passageway seems to go on and on forever and she becomes increasingly anxious and afraid.
But finally she sees the sun shining through the opening at the end. Just like the raven said.

They're almost there!

The two of them squeeze through the hole into the open. They can already see the river.
But their sense of relief doesn't last long. By the time they spot the hunters, it's too late.

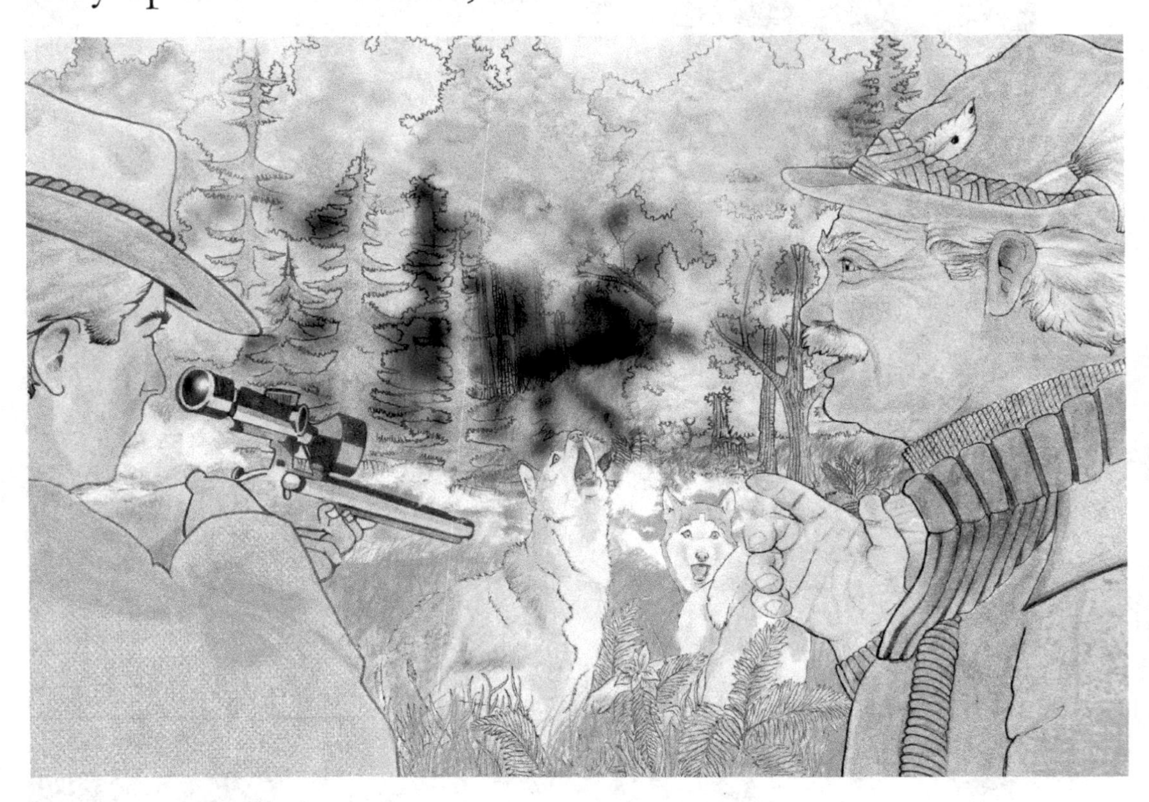

One of the two hunters already has his tranquilliser gun at the ready. When Abby sees this she begins to yap and bark as loud as she can. And although wolves don't normally bark, Tala joins in and she and Abby bark loudly together in unison.

The older hunter, a plump, easy-going man, bursts out laughing and shouts to his friend, “Don’t shoot, whatever you do. Those are two of the huskies from the top of the mountain. They’ve probably just run off and are enjoying a bit of fun in the woods. I told you there aren’t any wolves here. We’d better let the owners know where their dogs are.”

Abby and Tala run off at lightning speed and hide among the trees. Tala looks Abby firmly in the eyes. “Abby,” she says, “I don’t know how to thank you. Your idea to start barking saved us and thankfully you huskies seem to be pretty well known around here.”

But Abby doesn’t want Tala’s thanks yet. First, she has to help her new friend cross to the other side of the river.

Abby knows a nearby spot where they can cross safely thanks to large stones in the water. She, herself, has crossed the river there many times when she’s out walking with Susan.

But when they get to the spot, Tala hesitates. She is too afraid to cross the river. She remembers falling into the water and the pain of hitting her head. Abby bravely goes first, reassuring Tala that she can do it too. With Abby's encouragement and support, Tala finally plucks up the courage to walk over the stepping stones.

They reach the other side safely and without being spotted. When Tala looks into the forest her heart jumps for joy. Her brother is running towards her. He hadn't dared to cross the river, but he had waited here

for his sister all this time. They greet each other happily and Tala introduces Abby to her brother.
But now the time has come for them to say goodbye. Tala thanks Abby from the bottom of her heart and assures her she is the bravest, most courageous dog ever.
Overwhelmed by Tala's words, Abby bows her head modestly and wishes them both a fast, safe return to their pack. Tala and her brother set off on their somewhat longer walk home.

Abby runs home as fast as her legs will carry her. Hopefully no one has noticed how long she's been away. Maybe she'll even make it back in time for dinner. Luckily, she knows the way back and in no time at all she reaches the garden fence.
Just as she's cautiously squeezing through the hole, she hears Susan calling her name. All the huskies are standing in front of their bowls and tucking into their food. Abby runs over to join them. "Hey, little sleepyhead," says Susan, laughing. "You almost missed your dinner."

A short time after the dogs have finished eating, the gate bell rings. Curious to see who is there, all the huskies run down to look followed by James. Standing at the gate is the plump, friendly hunter who wants to let the family know where the two missing huskies are. Abby lingers in the background, hoping the hunter doesn't recognise her. With a puzzled expression on his face, James thanks the hunter but tells him that all the dogs are here, none are missing. The hunter scratches his head in bemusement. Then a wide grin spreads over his face and he says his goodbyes.

A short while later Abby is back lying on top of her kennel thinking about her unforgettable adventure. She hopes with all her heart that Tala and her brother have made it safely back to their pack. Suddenly the raven flies down and lands next to Abby. Delighted to see him, she says, "Hello, Mr Raven. How nice to see you again." "Hello, brave Abby," he caws. "I'm happy to see you again too. I came because I have something to tell you. The two wolves survived their journey back to their pack unharmed. I accompanied them on their way home and the whole pack, and your friend Tala in particular, asked me to send you their thanks and best wishes."

Abby woofs in delight and gives the raven a big, sloppy lick.

Somewhat embarrassed, the raven takes his leave.

"I have to go, dear Abby, but I'm sure we'll meet again soon."

Abby is happy and relieved knowing that her new friends are safe and sound.

The hole in the fence will stay her little secret, even if she's had enough adventures for the time being. She's certainly in no hurry to run off again. But who knows, maybe one day …

ABBY

Illustrated by Theresa Werner

www.theresa-werner.jimdo.com

Susanne Wolfgramm was born in Brühl near Cologne in 1966. After leaving school, she trained as a bank clerk and worked in that profession for many years. Her son was born in 1999, and several years later the first huskies came into her life. She, her son and her husband now share their home with several huskies and a wolfhound. Since her early childhood, Susanne has had a passion for language and writing. Inspired by her huskies, she decided to write a book. She has fond memories of the time when her now 21-year-old son was a little boy and she spent hours each evening reading stories to him. And so she immediately knew she wanted to write a children's book with her husky Abby as the hero. Furthermore, it has always been of great importance to Susanne that the stories she tells teach children positive values and, at the same time, entertain the adults reading to children.
Susanne Wolfgramm and her family currently live in Hürth but spend all their free time in their second home in the mountains of Germany's Eifel region.

www.susanne-wolfgramm.de

Titles previously published by Susanne Wolfgramm:

Ein Husky-Mädchen namens Abby
Alleine auf Tour
ISBN 978-3-7392-9727-9

Ein Husky-Mädchen namens Abby
Abby rettet Groß und Klein
ISBN 978-3-7431-5639-5

Ein Husky-Mädchen namens Abby
Abby und die Labradore
ISBN 978-3-7528-3754-4

Der kleine T-Rex Tom
Abenteuer in der Kreidezeit
ISBN 978-3-7412-4810-8

For further information on these books and to view photographs of Abby visit

www.susanne-wolfgramm.de

CPSIA information can be obtained
at www.ICGtesting.com
Printed in the USA
LVHW100926180521
687738LV00012B/638